# PERSEPHONE PLUS

## STEVIE RAE CAUSEY

# Stevie Rae Causey

# CHAPTER 1

"You worry too much, Seph."

Persephone sighed as she used the full-length mirror to steal a glance over her shoulder at her partner. On the bed, Adonis hunched over their sketchbook. Her eyes traveled over the black and violet hoodie and leggings before shifting back to their serene face. "I have to worry for both of us...because *you* don't worry enough."

She pulled her newly dyed hair back from her face and examined her eyeliner. Winter was one of her favorite phases. Dark clothes, dark hair, dark makeup, and especially the nail polish made her feel a pang of nostalgia. In the past, warriors had adorned their fingers with obsidian hues before battle. Some of the old traditions still existed in the modern world.

As she dabbed at the corners of her eyes, Adonis warned, "If you don't leave it alone, you're going to smear it."

"Is that something you learned in art?" she teased as she turned to face them.

They delicately erased an area that had been worked so much the paper was beginning to visibly wear. "Eh." They shrugged with a lopsided grin. "Those who can't do teach."

She abandoned the touch-up efforts and glanced away. As she did, the manilla envelope on Adonis' nightstand caught her eye and her stomach sank.

"Nervous?" Adonis asked.

Persephone nodded. "Have you read it yet?"

"No," they said casually, "but I know what it says."

"Addy! You've had it for three days." She picked up the file. It felt heavy in her hands and on her heart. "How are you supposed to get her to sign if you haven't even read it?"

A wave of self-doubt rushed over her. The agreement was legally solid; she'd made sure of that. If everything went as planned, they might finally have a way out of this whole mess. If it didn't...

"I'm gonna miss the red hair," Adonis said, changing the subject.

"You'll get used to the change." She sat down on the bed beside them and they both went silent.

Before Zeus had banished them, Adonis had spent her winter phase with another partner. It wasn't that Persephone expected monogamy. That would be unfair given that she was married to someone else.

Adonis wrapped their arms around her and kissed her forehead. "I'll love you in every phase you let me."

"That's the problem." Persephone pulled away. "It's not up to me." As she searched their face, Adonis' gaze slid aside and she followed it to the calendar on the wall.

They had highlighted the days they had left together. Today was circled in red, marking the last day before campus closed for winter break. It was also the last day Seph and Adonis had together. The rest of the month was shaded an ominous black, representing the uncertainty of their future.

As the only natural-born mortal, Adonis had the least amount of representation in the dispute Persephone was hoping to settle with Aphrodite.

"It's not fair," she said aloud. "but my feelings for you don't change with the seasons either. You know that, right?"

"Zeus doesn't really care about fair," Adonis said sourly. "He just doesn't want to have to deal with any of it."

"Can you blame him? Aphrodite is impossible to work with." Even if it was true, she regretted the words as soon as they came out of her mouth.

"That is *not* fair." Adonis rarely became cross with Persephone, but when they did, it was bound to be about the Goddess of Love. "She's learned a lot in our time here. You don't give her enough credit."

Persephone rolled her eyes. "I don't see how you can excuse her so easily. There was no reason for her to have a problem with the first agreement. You were spending all your extra time with her anyway."

"Look, can we not fight during our last hours together?" they pleaded and placed a hand over hers.

The tension melted at their touch. "Is it always going to be this complicated?" Her eyes locked on that manilla envelope, almost forgotten in the argument, and she struggled to find hope.

"We'll figure it out." They took the file from her and put it in their book bag. "It's a good plan, Seph. You worry about Hades. Let me worry about Aphrodite. Now come on. We're gonna be late to class."

As she shouldered her backpack, she couldn't help but feel like it was just a little heavier than usual. That weight only grew as they walked across the university courtyard. Every step felt like it was leading her closer to an ultimatum she wasn't willing to accept. What if Aphrodite decided she wanted Adonis all to herself? It was one thing to come up with a good plan—pen and paper rarely argued back—but she had way less control over how it would be executed. She hated feeling powerless.

She held the door open for Adonis when they reached the fine arts building. She wasn't anxious to face the other students trying to make it to class. She just disliked the crowded hallways. Artificial light, sneakers squeaking on scuffed floors, the overwhelming mix of perfumes, sweat, and stress—it felt like a prison. The Goddess of Spring was meant for frolicking in fields.

On their first day over a year ago, Hades had said, "This place is beneath you." He'd picked up a ball of notebook paper that had rebounded off the rim of the garbage can after being tossed from an unknown location and stared at it with a deep frown. "Hallways of crumpled dreams and forgotten erasers." The name still felt appropriate—as juxtaposed as they were: the Goddess of Spring and the God of Death.

The memory made her smile.

They reached the atrium, where the crowd thinned as students filed down separate hallways toward their first class. All except for a group of rich kids known as the Pearls. They stood in a half circle looking down their noses as other students walked by. Persephone wanted nothing more than to turn and take the first door out of their view. Where there were Pearls, there was bound to be—

"Hey, Aphrodite," Adonis said casually.

The Goddess of Love snapped her fingers as she sauntered toward them, glaring at Persephone before turning a sickeningly sweet smile at Adonis. All chatter in the atrium ceased.

"Last day before break," Aphrodite said, as if it was some privileged information she was bestowing. She had always considered her presence itself to be a gift to the mortals around her, an approach that had worked out quite well for her in the college social hierarchy.

Aphrodite's cronies looked to her for direction as Persephone and Adonis approached.

"To class." She waved a hand. After the crowd dispersed, she batted her thick eyelashes at Adonis. "Any fun plans?"

"You know I don't," Adonis said flatly.

Aphrodite set her eyes on Persephone next. "And you? Back to your"—she dropped her voice— "*husband?*" She emphasized the last word and cast her gaze around the atrium in mock concern.

Heat crept up Persephone's cheeks. She wasn't ashamed of her choices normally, but there was something about this mortal body that couldn't help but fall victim to the venomous judgement in Aphrodite's voice. "At least all of my partners know about one another," she shot back wryly.

"Ah yes, it must have been a bitch for Hades, having to raise his replacement. How ever did you get him to agree to that?" Aphrodite smirked at a blow well-struck.

"Says the person who tried to lock a child in a chest because it was burdensome." A righteous anger welled up in her chest as she recalled the day Hades had pulled the wailing infant from the prison. "What did you expect him to do, let Adonis die?"

Aphrodite's eyes went wide as their remaining peers paused to rubberneck at the drama.

Adonis didn't have to say anything out loud, but Persephone could feel them thinking, *Not cool, Seph.* And they were right. Poking at old wounds wasn't going to move any of them forward.

Clouds gathered in the goddess's eyes and Persephone got the sense that the limits of their mortal bodies were the only thing keeping the entire campus from being demolished to rubble.

"Be careful, daughter of Demeter," Aphrodite warned through a forced smile.

Persephone dropped her gaze and kept her mouth shut. Aphrodite's message was loud and clear: her mother's status would not help her here.

Adonis stepped in on her behalf. "That's enough."

When Persephone looked up, she saw Aphrodite's posture soften. The tension in the air dissipated and the crowd resumed their scramble to make it to class on time.

"Aww, Addy, you know I'm only having fun." Aphrodite's smile turned into a sultry pout. "Human life is *so* boring. You can't blame me for wanting to spice things up a little."

"I can if it gets the rest of us in more trouble." Their voice was soft but firm.

Aphrodite stepped in closer and wrapped her arms around their neck. "Oh come on, you can't say you're not excited to get back to normal."

Persephone's shoulders crawled toward her ears as the tension between the two grew. Seeing Aphrodite fling herself shamelessly at Adonis made Persephone want to punch the pouty smile right off of her face.

Adonis did it for her...with words instead of a fist. "What is normal to you, Aphrodite?" They pulled out of her embrace.

"What's your problem?"
Aphrodite demanded.

Persephone held her breath.
Aphrodite didn't handle rejection
well.

"My problem?!" Adonis had never
been this angry at Aphrodite before,
and their voice was starting to draw
attention. "You're not taking this
seriously. We've already been given
one ruling and it wasn't good
enough, and that stunt you pulled
with Orpheus put all of us at risk."

Persephone felt a twinge of
satisfaction watching Aphrodite
answer for her disrespect. Calliope

had divided the year equally between the three of them, with Aphrodite and Persephone each having four months with Adonis before they spent the remaining four months as they pleased.

Aphrodite's retribution was fatal. Persephone did *not* look forward to processing the souls in the Underworld when this was all over. So. Much. Paperwork.

The echo of Adonis' squeaking sneakers bounced off the walls as they spun to make a quick exit, fists clenched at their sides. "Come on, Seph," they called over their shoulder. They didn't wait to see whether she followed.

Persephone wished she could hit the restart button on this whole day and it had barely started. As she moved to catch up with Adonis, Aphrodite heckled her one last time.

"I almost feel bad for you, Persephone. Your winter break is going to be Hell."

# Chapter 2

It took all day for Adonis to cool down, but cool down they did, much to Persephone's relief. She had no love for Aphrodite, but she couldn't stand to see Adonis torn up about her either. Not just because they needed Aphrodite's signature on the agreement. Adonis' physical beauty was a thing of legends, but even more beautiful to Persephone was their forgiving nature. Seeing them hold onto a grudge against a partner felt like a violation of their values, even if that partner *was* Aphrodite.

Persephone hadn't seen Aphrodite since that morning in the atrium. She'd been absent in gym, not that it was all that unusual for her to skip that class. The Goddess of Love had been mortified when she realized mortal bodies sweat.

Still, the pit in Persephone's stomach had grown heavier as the day went on. How could she have let her mouth get the best of her? Now her whole plan could be ruined just because she couldn't keep her composure during an argument.

An even bigger fear took root in her mind as the day wore on: what if she'd sabotaged the plan on purpose? A part of her felt protective of Adonis' and it made sense that it would spill into jealousy given their dynamic. In fact, as she thought about it, she wondered if it was the same competitive streak in her that made her want to 'win' Adonis' affection. She'd have to work harder to manage her reaction, or she'd have no one to blame but herself for

Adonis' fate. In this situation, restraint was her most powerful tool.

As Persephone thought herself in circles, her worry turned to dread.

She couldn't bear the tension any longer as Adonis walked her to her final class of the day. "You're going to have to figure things out with Aphrodite for this to work, you know?" she said as they approached the biology classroom. This was the last chance they had to see each other until Athena's ruling was given, and she hated to waste it fighting, but all of this would be for nothing if she didn't speak up now.

Adonis jerked their head, flipping their bangs out of their eyes and glanced away to avoid eye contact. The attempt must have backfired because their expression turned sour. "You first." They nodded toward a desk in the back corner of the classroom before kissing her cheek. "See you soon."

Persephone watched as Adonis disappeared into a sea of other students and whispered a desperate prayer to herself: *Please don't let that be the last thing we say to each other.*

She sighed and wandered to the back corner of the classroom where she dropped her bookbag on the floor and sank into her chair as heavily as her heart felt.

"Jeez, nice to see you too, lab partner." Hades said without looking up from the text he was sending.

"It's not you," she said defensively. "Although, you moping in the corner like a kicked puppy while I say goodbye wasn't helping."

"They don't have to rub it in my face. Everyone can see them walk you to class." He hit send and set the phone on the table.

She threw her hands up in frustration. "And they can see me go home with you for all I care!"

Around them, the other students had begun to stare. Hades' phone buzzed on the desk.

A burning feeling crept up Persephone's face as he picked it up. His jaw tightened in response to the message he was reading.

"Are you even paying attention?" Persephone's patience was wearing thin.

Hades swallowed, took a breath, and his face softened. "Sorry, work stuff."

"Let the intern handle it," she chided.

"Do you even know what kind of mess is waiting for us back home?"

"Can we not do this right now? I'm really excited about the final and I just want to get through winter break before we worry about work.

"Only you would be excited about a biology final," Hades said with a smile that actually reached his eyes. He put the phone away.

"Not just any biology." As she pulled out her notes, the excitement rose in her chest, coursing through her arms until her fingers tingled. "*Plant* biology."

"Oh, yes, much different," Hades teased.

Persephone leaned into him and playfully nudged him with her elbow. "Hey, you wouldn't even be passing this class if you weren't married to the daughter of Demeter."

"Fair enough," he acquiesced.

"All right, all right, settle down!" their instructor called as he entered the room. "You have ten minutes to review before the final exam. Use it wisely."

Persephone opened the book, though she didn't need the review. The test would be a welcome distraction from her internal battle. Winter break started in one hour, and then the countdown would really begin.

# Chapter 3

As Hades drove up the mountain to his cabin, Persephone thought about everything that had changed in the last year. Of all of them, Hades had changed the least. She wondered what strings her husband had pulled to make that happen.

On their third day together, it snowed enough to play. Persephone pulled a reluctant Hades out the door.

"The Lord of the Underworld does not play in the snow," he said indignantly.

"The Lord of the Underworld will do as his wife wishes." She laughed and tugged harder.

Hours later, the two stared proudly at their three-headed snow sculpture.

"A fine likeness," Hades said.

"I miss Cerberus." Persephone patted the side of the great, icy beast.

Hades wrapped his hands around her waist and rested his chin on her shoulder. "He misses you too."

"Do you ever get sick of living two lives?" she asked, and she leaned her head against his.

"I do," he said. "But it will all be over soon, and then we can go back our kingdom together.

"Have you read the paperwork?" Persephone had avoided the question long enough.

His grip around her waist loosened. "Do we have to do this now?"

"When else are we going to talk about it, Hades? Mediation is tomorrow." She pulled away from his embrace.

"Can you not be with me, *just me,* for a few days? Is it really that terrible for you?"

"That isn't fair."

"Fair? Is that what you were worried about when you wrote the agreement? Being fair to everyone?! Yes, I read it Persephone. Our relationship isn't some playground toy—"

"Don't," Persephone warned. "Don't finish that sentence."

He abruptly headed for the cabin.

"You can't walk away, either!" she called to him. "We promised not to walk away from each other."

Hades turned reluctantly, and Persephone's fear melted when she realized why he'd wanted to run. The God of the Underworld clenched and unclenched his jaw as silent tears flowed down his cheeks.

Persephone waited. She wanted desperately to go to him and offer comfort, but this was something he had to move through on his own; all she could do was stand firm and wait for him to accept all of her.

After what seemed like an eternity, he exhaled an icy breath. His fists stayed clenched and shook as he inhaled again. "You're right," he said. "I'm sorry, Seph. I just don't know what to do with all of this sometimes. It's hard to see you change while I remain forever frozen in time. It's even more torturous to watch you change in the arms of someone else."

"The phases I move through are independent of the partner I share them with." She closed the distance between them and wiped a tear from his cheek. "I'm not asking you to watch me change with someone else. I'm asking you to hold my hand while we create something new together. You will always be my husband. My heart will always know yours."

He nodded and finally glanced up to meet her eyes. When he shakily exhaled and hugged her, she found hope. Not just for mediation, but for all the seasons to come.

# Chapter 4

The elevator dinged, signaling that Persephone had reached the sixty-third floor of Olympus Corp. She exited into a reception area, empty except for the secretary behind the desk who barely paid her any attention. She wondered if she was the first to arrive.

"Olympus Corp, please hold." The receptionist held her hand over the receiver. "They're waiting for you," she said and motioned toward a set of large, double doors.

Inside, Athena sat at a large, marble table. On the other side, Hades sat on one end and Aphrodite the other. In the middle two more chairs sat empty.

"Good afternoon," Athena said and motioned to one of the empty chairs. "Welcome to your mediation. Please have a seat."

"Do you have to say that to everyone?" Aphrodite complained.

"It's part of the process," Athena responded evenly.

"Well can we at least get the process started? I have things to attend to."

"We can't start without Adonis. You know that." Athena was all business today.

Persephone hoped that was a good sign. She chose the seat nearest to Hades, and he greeted her with a kiss.

Aphrodite folded her arms and slouched in her chair. "Let's make it fast when they get here. I don't want drama to take up too much of my vacay."

Hades took the bait. "We wouldn't even *have* to be here if it weren't for you."

Aphrodite feigned disinterest by pulling out a nail file and running it across the tips of her fading manicure. "You're just upset your wife decided to press the issue rather than let go of her playmate."

"Careful, Aphrodite," Athena warned. "Adonis' rights are protected under Medusa's Mortal Protection Act. If the group cannot come to an amicable agreement, Adonis will be released back to their original, mortal life for good."

Persephone swallowed the gravelly lump in her throat. Its weight rested heavily in her gut.

Though Aphrodite's face flushed, she didn't dare challenge Athena's authority. "They could have been grandfathered in," she mumbled.

A prickly heat crept up the back of Persephone's neck in response. She desperately wanted to call out Aphrodite's shitty attitude. If Athena noticed, she gave no sign.

"Human rights aren't really her thing," Adonis said cheekily as they made their entrance. They didn't wait for Athena's scripted welcome to take their seat.

For a moment, the rest of the room faded from Persephone's awareness. Her heart soared when Adonis looked her way only to fall back into the present moment as she watched Aphrodite take their hand. Doubt flooded her mind. Could she really stand to send Adonis into the arms of someone like that?

*Don't infantilize them,* she mentally chastised herself. Adonis was more than capable of making their own choices, and her relationship with them was separate from Aphrodite's. *And, therefore, none of my business.*

She slowly exhaled and silently hoped, pressing her feet into the floor to ground herself. How she wished for the feel of grass beneath her bare feet rather than the feel of sneakers against musty, low-rise carpet. Outside, it began to snow.

"I trust everyone is familiar with the agreement. Or should I go through it again?" Athena asked as she handed out forms.

Everyone nodded.

Athena addressed Adonis, "And you agree to the loss of your four months in favor of a more amicable agreement?"

"Being forced to choose between the people I love at the expense of our relationships is not a freedom. Let them each feel secure in their equal treatment by me."

Persephone reached over from her chair and squeezed Addys' hand. On their other side, Aphrodite did the same. For a moment, they locked eyes with the Goddess of Love, and Persephone thought she saw a small smile flash across Aphrodite's face before she glanced away.

"Aphrodite?" Athena motioned to the recording device on the table.

Persephone couldn't help but get some measure of amusement from the way Aphrodite squirmed at the sound of her old rival saying her name.

"The records require verbal consent as well as your signature."

Adonis squeezed Aphrodite's hand tighter. "It's not a loss, babe."

When Aphrodite sighed, Athena raised an eyebrow and indicated the recorder again.

"Fi—Yes. I consent."

Aphrodite turned to the other end of the table. "Hades?"

The temperature of the room dropped significantly as all eyes shifted to Hades. He had never been much of a public speaker. Nor did he particularly enjoy sharing his feelings. And here he was, being asked to do both for an audience. Not just any audience: a judge.

Persephone's heart ached for the position he was in, for what she was asking of him. She placed her hand over his icy fingers and sent him the feel of a warm, Spring day. His skin warmed beneath hers and the tension slowly melted from his frame.

"I thought sharing her would shatter me." He paused and Persephone held her breath, expecting Aphrodite to make some snide response, but none came. The entire room had been moved to silence. "Now I see she's not mine to share. That she shares herself freely. I would never strip her of that power. My love for her does not waiver, no matter her phase. I am content to love the parts she chooses to share during our time together."

He signed the contract and slid it across the table. Not to be outdone, Aphrodite followed, signing her name in broad flowery strokes. Adonis and Persephone slid their pre-signed agreements across the table in unison.

"And, thus, the whole is born of the fragmented," Athena said as she stuffed the forms into a manilla envelope and sealed it.

It was done. At least unofficially.

What next?" Hades asked.

"Now, we wait," Athena said. "But I see no reason for Zeus to reject the ruling. Your banishment appeal should be processed in the next five years."

"That soon, huh?" Hades said sullenly.

"I don't make the rules," Athena said. "I just enforce them." She looked around the room, and some of the sternness seemed to melt. "Think of it as a well-earned vacation."

"Oh, come on, are you really *that* anxious to get back to work?" Persephone replied.

Hades smiled sheepishly. "No, I was just hoping to be gone before grades were posted."

# Chapter 5

Persephone was the only one to linger when the others dispersed. Normally, she loved a good transition. But this one had a reverence to it, and that was a feeling she wanted to hold onto a little longer. She stared awhile out the large window.

Warmth spread throughout her chest as she looked out at the

modern world in a way that was full of promise. Spring would be back soon, and so would she. For now, she would relax in the peace that came with accepting the impending transition.

"I'll admit, even I am surprised you were able to pull this off." Athena's voice pulled her from her thoughts. The Goddess of Wisdom finished some paperwork and slid it into another manilla envelope before pressing a call button on her desk.

A beam of light appeared next to Persephone, and she stepped aside to make room for the Messenger God.

"You know where this goes, I assume?" Athena pressed the envelope into Hermes' hands.

"All the way to the top!" he replied with a wink before disappearing in another beam of light.

Athena turned back to Persephone. "Never thought I would see the day Aphrodite would agree to share."

"I'm afraid you've missed the point entirely, then."

Athena raised an eyebrow and Persephone's heart skipped a beat. Did she really just tell the Goddess of Wisdom she'd missed the point? *Well,* she thought, *I've already committed.*

"No one of us owns the other. The only thing we can share is our truest selves."

"An interesting strategy, nonetheless," Athena replied with a wry smile.

They looked out the window together, through the clouds and down to a world that was changing in ways even the gods didn't comprehend.

Persephone took a deep breath. "Perhaps it's time we fought different battles."

Athena smiled. "I see wisdom in your battle strategy." She leaned in to hug Persephone. "Your mother sends her regards." And then she faded into light, the same way as Hermes.

Persephone's phone buzzed. As she read Hades' text, she beamed.

*"Hey, we're going out for lunch— all of us. Wanna come?"*

She couldn't think of a better way to spend the rest of their mortal time together.

# **Acknowledgments**

THANKS FOR READING!

I HAVE MET SOME AMAZING PEOPLE THROUGH MY READERSHIP THE PAST COUPLE OF YEARS AND I CAN'T WAIT TO LAUNCH INTO WHAT COMES NEXT!

IF YOU ENJOYED THIS STORY, PLEASE CONSIDER LEAVING A REVIEW. REVIEWS HELP US FIND MORE READERS, AND MORE READERS HELP US WRITE MORE BOOKS!

# Stevie's Other Works

**THE AMASAI RISING QUARTET:**

**THE WEAVER'S SON SERIES**

# About the Author

Stevie Rae Causey is an author, podcaster, guest speaker, and general nerd living in the Pacific Northwest. Special interests include relational psychology, symbolism, hiking, and dogs. May very well just be a series of coping mechanisms in a trench coat masquerading as human.

# WANT TO KNOW MORE ABOUT AUTHOR LIFE? LISTEN TO MY PODCAST WITH GRETCHEN SB